THIS BOOK BELONGS TO

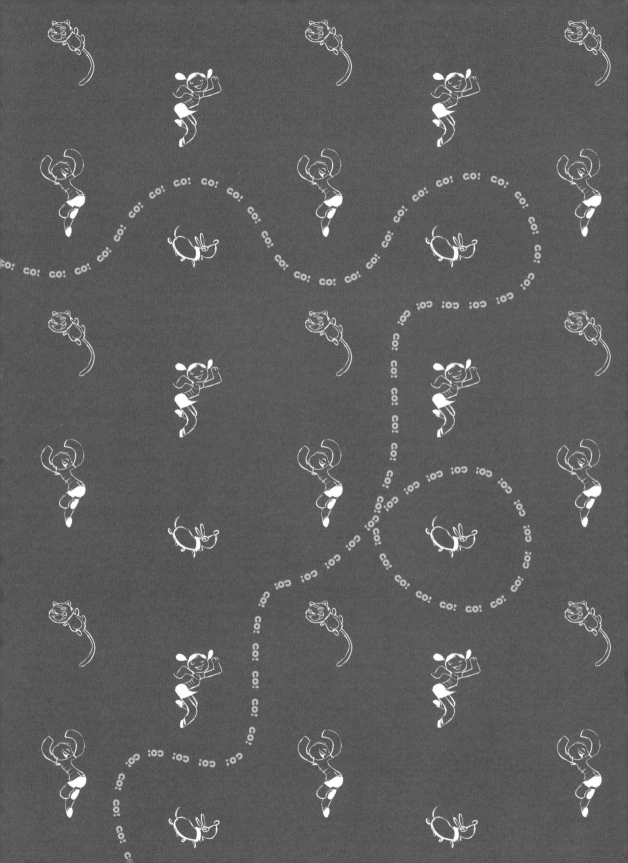

ILLUSTRATIONS
by
PASCAL
CAMPION

KIDS

SIMON & SCHUSTER

NEW YORK
LONDON
TORONTO
SYDNEY

GO!

THEY
MIGHT
BE
GIANTS

MAKERS *of* MUSIC

Also by

THEY MIGHT BE GIANTS

BED, BED, BED

Simon & Schuster
1230 Avenue of the Americas
New York, NY 10020

Copyright © 2009
by They Might Be Giants

All rights reserved, including the right to
reproduce this book or portions thereof
in any form whatsoever. For information
address Simon & Schuster Subsidiary Rights
Department, 1230 Avenue of the Americas,
New York, NY 10020.

First Simon & Schuster hardcover edition
November 2009
SIMON & SCHUSTER
and colophon are registered trademarks
of Simon & Schuster, Inc.

For information about special discounts
for bulk purchases, please contact
Simon & Schuster Special Sales at
1-866-506-1949 or
business@simonandschuster.com.

The Simon & Schuster Speakers Bureau
can bring authors to your live event. For
more information or to book an event
contact the Simon & Schuster Speakers
Bureau at 1-866-248-3049 or visit our
website at www.simonspeakers.com.

Designed by Melissa Jun

Manufactured in China

10 9 8 7 6 5 4 3 2 1

Library of Congress
Cataloging-in-Publication Data
Kids go! / They Might Be Giants ;
[illustrations by Pascal Campion].
        p.   cm.
    1. Children's songs, English—
    United States—Texts. 2. Songs.
      I. Campion, Pascal.
      II. Title.
    PZ8.3.T265 Go 2009
    782.42 E—dc22   2009019668

ISBN 978-0-7432-7275-9

KIDS GO!

{ There is a special
DVD
just for you
in the
back of this book
with an
animated video
of this story.
Play it now
if you want to
sing along! }

Ready?

HEY,

kid!

NOW'S THE TIME TO STAND UP

MOVE

YOUR

LEGS

and raise up

both of
your arms
and
wave them
in the air

Get up off the couch and **GO**

Get up
off
your chair
and
GO!

GO! GO

If
you're
HEARING
this
song

then **IT'S TIME** to jump along

THEN

GET

UP

NOW

AND

go!

go!

GO!

Move like a monkey

GO!

STAND
on
one
leg

and
then
STAND
on
the
other
leg

and then
pick up
both
legs
and

YOU'RE

FLOATING

IN

THE

It's
time
to
GO

Get up
off
the
couch
and
GO

JUMP UP FROM THE

FLOOR AND GO!

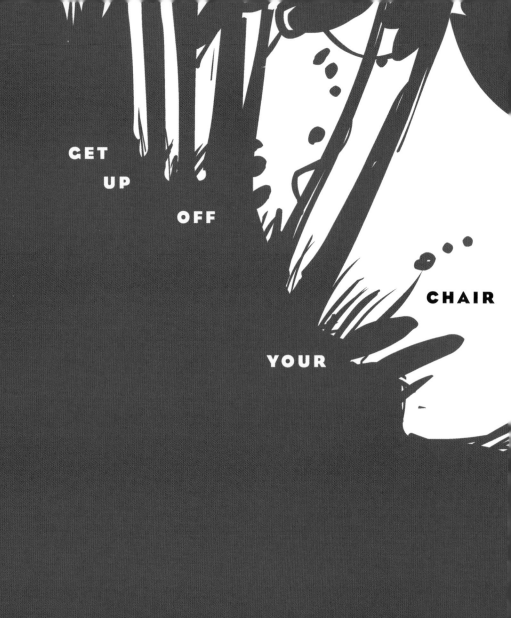

GET

UP

OFF

YOUR

CHAIR

go!

AND

go!

go!

You should already be jumping like

A **JACK-IN-THE-BOX** *so, go!*

MOVE LIKE A MONKEY

Move like a jumping bean

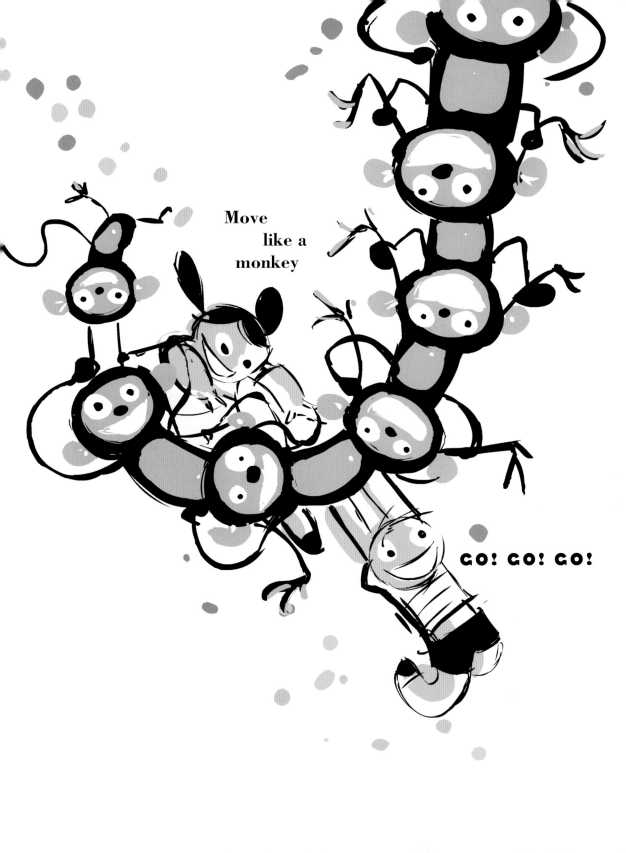

And if
you're
hearing
this
song

then
it's time
to
jump
along

MOVE

M O V E

A   M O

L I K E

N K E Y

Go!

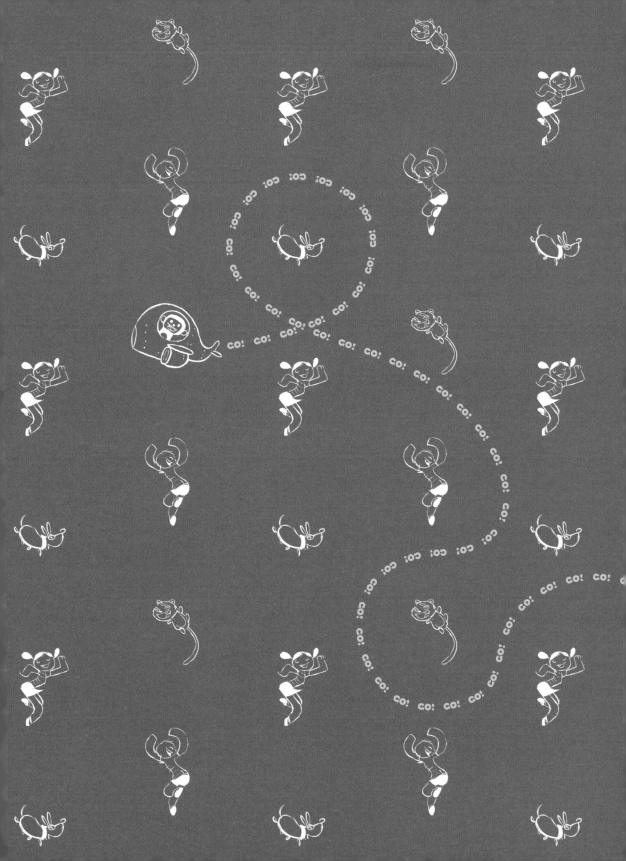

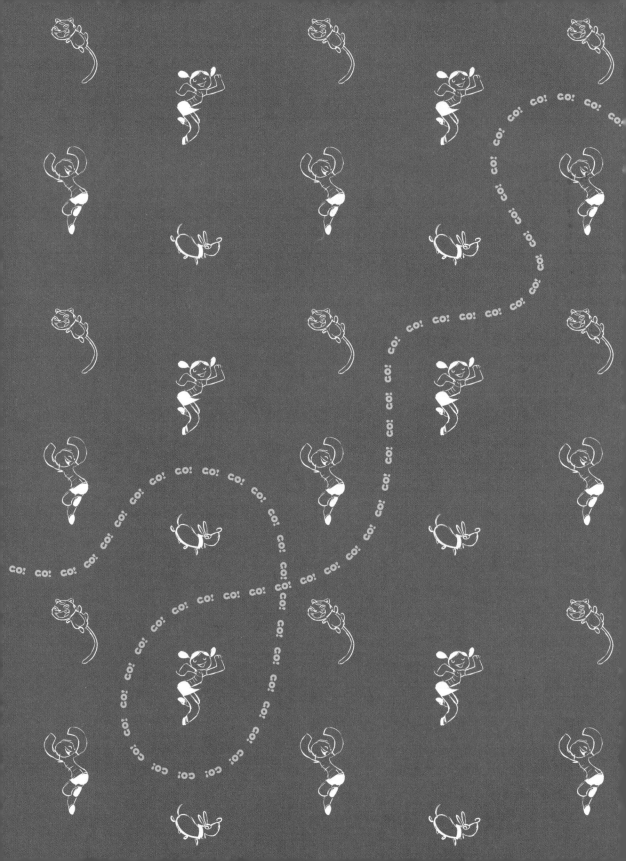